Hardback - ISBN 13: 978-1-963016-47-5
E-Book - ISBN 13: 978-1-963016-48-2

Published in the United States of America.

Joan Murray Ministries &
Seeds of Hope Worldwide Missions

26340 FM 1736
Waller, TX 77484

281-398-2501

As Ishmael rounded the corner, he heard music. The servants were busy preparing the party for his little brother, Isaac.

As the guests began to arrive, Ishmael went to play with his four-year-old brother.

Sitting beside Isaac, Ishmael watched the guests talk and laugh among themselves.

Turning to Isaac, Ishmael began to tickle him. Isaac squealed with laughter.

Isaac yelled, "Ishmael, stop," as he tried to escape from his brother.

Ishmael said, Isaac, you are such a baby, grinning at his brother.

Sarah joined them, wearing a stern look on her face.
"Ishmael," Sarah yelled. "Why are you bothering your
baby brother, Isaac?"
"I'm only teasing him," Ishmael said.
"Leave him alone and go to your room," Sarah said sternly.
Looking at her and then at Isaac, Ishmael went to his room.

The next day, Ishmael watched as his mother began packing their clothes. "Mommy, where are we going?"
Hagar, Ishmael's Mother, remained silent because she couldn't express her feelings or explain the situation in a way her son could understand.
She didn't understand it herself.
"Ishmael, we have to find a new home. We can no longer live here," Hagar explained.

"But I already have a home," Ishmael shouted.
"Yes, son, but...I don't know how to explain it."
"I don't want to leave my home, Mom." Ishmael began to cry.
"I know, son, I know."

Ishmael cried harder, "Mommy, please stop packing."
Ishmael's mother, displaying great inner strength, gathered
him into her arms as she tried to comfort him.
Looking down to hide her tears, Hagar prayed.
"Lord, help me explain this so he can understand."
Her heart was heavy with the weight of the situation. "I
don't want Ishmael to be scared or sad."

"Ishmael, look at me," Hagar said.

Hagar took a deep breath of courage and said, "Son, we no longer get to live here."

"What do you mean?" eight-year-old Ishmael asked? "I have my own room," he said with a whimper.

"My son, Mamma Sarah, told us to move out."

"Move where? We live with her and my new brother." Ishmael exclaimed.

"She wants us to go and live with our other family." said
Hagar.
"But why?" cried Ishmael! "I don't know the other family," he
said as he laid his head on her lap.
"Yes, son, but I do. You just haven't met them yet, but you
will soon.
"Ishmael, you have a grandma and grandpa and many uncles,
aunts, and cousins.
"You will have great fun with them!" Hagar exclaimed.

Ishmael felt sad but didn't know why.
"Momma, I want to see my father."
As tears ran silently down her face, Hagar couldn't find the
words to tell him his father also wanted them to leave.

"You will see your father soon, son.
"In the meantime, you have a great big Daddy who has been watching over you and me for a long time," Hagar reassured, emphasizing the presence and guidance of God.
Who is my new Daddy, Momma?
Hagar pointed to the sky.
"You see how big the sky is, Ishmael?"
"Yes, Momma."
"Your new Daddy lives there, and He has always been with you."

"When you were in my tummy, I met Him. He told me to call you Ishmael."
"He did?" Ishmael squeaked. "He gave me my name?" "Yes," his Momma said with a smile.
Ishmael's radiant smile lit up as he stared joyfully at his Momma.

"Would you like to know what your name means, son?"
"What, Momma?" It means "God hears." "It's a special name because it reminds us that God always hears us, even when we're sad or scared," Hagar explained.
"You know what, son?"
"God hears you right now."
"God is your new Daddy; you can talk to Him anytime."
"Ishmael, do you understand?"
"Yes, Momma, my new Daddy, has always been with me."

"Momma, how do I talk to my new Daddy?"
Hagar smiled, remembering the first time she talked to God.
Smiling at Ishmael, she folded her hands together.
"Son, this is how you talk to your new Daddy."
Kneeling down beside her son, Hagar taught him how to talk to Daddy God.
"Son, after praying to Daddy, be quiet and listen to Him."

"Daddy God, this is Ishmael. Are you listening to me?"
"Do you hear me?" Listening intently, Ishmael heard a quiet whisper. "Yes, Ishmael, I hear you, my son."
"Momma, Momma! Daddy God called me son." Ishmael beamed from cheek to cheek.

Smiling with relief, Hagar hugs Ishmael, whispering. "Thank you, Daddy God."

The next day, Abraham, Ishmael's father, gave Hagar bread and water and sent them away.

Hagar lost her way as they traveled, and the bread and water ran out.

"Momma," said Ishmael, "I'm tired and thirsty. May I have a cup of water?"

Hagar began to panic because she had run out of water and bread.

She didn't know what to tell her son. She was afraid. Sitting Ishmael down, she began to cry silently.

Ishmael began crying. "Momma, I'm hungry."
"I know, son, our new Daddy will take care of us.
Sad and afraid, Hagar slowly moved away as she watched her
son crying.

Suddenly, Hagar heard a voice from heaven.
"What's wrong, Hagar? I heard you and your son crying.
Don't be scared. Ishmael will have a big family, and I will
make him great!"
God opened Hagar's eyes wide, and she saw a well with
water.
She filled up her jug and gave water to Ishmael.
He drank until he was full. Ishmael beamed with joyfully at
his Momma.

"Ishmael, when you asked me for water, I had none to give you."
"We had run out of water."
"As you were crying, your new Daddy God sent a big angel to tell me He saw you crying."
"He told me not to be afraid and showed me the water well."
"Son, do you understand what I'm saying?"
"Yes, Momma. Daddy, God heard me crying. He's listening to me."
Hagar smiled, relieved that her son understood God was with them.

One day, Ishmael prayed, "Daddy God, I want to go home," he said.

He sat still and waited for an answer. Softly, Daddy God answered. "Soon, son, soon."

"I can hear Him! I can hear Him!" Ishmael shouted, looking into the sky!

Hagar smiled with relief because God showed Ishmael he was loved and heard.

One day, as they traveled, Hagar saw a town...

Touching Ishmael on the shoulders, she said, "Look, son, look.

That's our new home. Daddy God has guided us here."

Ishmael squinted his eyes trying to see the new place.

"Momma, I see it," he squealed.

Hagar laughed, filled with relief.

"Thank you, Daddy God, for getting us safely to our new home."

"Momma, will my father know where to find me?"
"Yes, son, he will know where to find you."
Looking into the sky, Hagar silently prayed.
"Daddy God, help my son. He misses his father."
Hagar waited to hear the answer.

Daddy God answered.
"I will be with Ishmael every day of his life."
"I will never leave his side."
"I will create a great nation out of him and his children."
"I will make him very GREAT!"

Arriving with Ishmael in the Desert of Beersheba,
Hagar found them a place to live.
Ishmael still missed his father and little brother, but
Daddy God filled his life with new friends.

As Ishmael got older, Daddy God stayed by his side.
He talked often to his new Daddy.
He had many friends to play with and had great fun.

Ishmael prayed that his father would visit and bring Isaac, his little brother.
One day, they came, and Ishmael was pleased to see them.
He showed them his new home, and they met his new friends.
Ishmael told his father and little brother, "I have a big new Daddy, God."

"My new Daddy God hears me when I pray and tells me things."
"What does He tell you, son, his father, Abraham asks?" That I am
His son," Ishmael answered with a grin.
"He talks to me when I pray to him, and I listen quietly."
"He has always been with me and Momma since we left home."

Looking into the sky, Ishmael said to Isaac, his little brother.
"My new Daddy lives there." Isaac gazed with big eyes into the sky.
"Wow, your new Daddy is big!" he exclaimed.
Nodding his head and with a big smile, Ishmael answered
" Yes He is!"

As their father, Abraham, watched his two sons gazing into the sky, He smiled.
Relief flooded his heart to see them talking, smiling, and laughing together.

"Thank you, Daddy God, for caring for Ishmael when I could not always be with him," said Abraham, with tears in his eyes.
Hagar smiled as she watched the boys talking and pointing into the sky.
She knew her son, Ishmael, was telling his brother Isaac about his big new Daddy God.
Joy filled her heart to see her son happy.

Hagar prayed.

"Thank you, Daddy God, for watching over my son and me."

"Thank you for filling his heart with love."

"Thank you for never leaving his side."

"He still misses his father, Abraham, but you have been a wonderful Daddy to him."

Psalm 27:10 - Even when my mother and Father forsake me, the Lord will receive me.

About the Author

Joan Murray is totally committed to helping people discover their destinies. She is the founder and CEO of Joan Murray Ministries and Seeds of Hope Worldwide Missions. Joan is dedicated to teaching, training, equipping and helping people who are in various life struggles. Joan is a minister, bible teacher, author, and missionary. She has traveled extensively throughout the United States and internationally sharing the gospel and serving the needs of the oppressed. She currently resides in Houston, Texas.

If you would like to know more about Joan Murray Ministries or Seeds of Hope Worldwide Missions, please get in touch with us at:
Joan Murray Ministries & Seeds Of Hope Worldwide Missions
26340 FM 1736
Waller, TX 77848
281-398-2504
email:jmmcontactus@gmail.com
website:joanmurrayministries.org
website: www.jemmuniquegifts.com

Changing Lives Through the Power and Truth of God's Word.